Yun
and the
Fire Dragon

Written by Charlotte Raby

Illustrated by Simona Sanfilippo

Chapter 1
The Magic Pearl

Yun sat by the lake. He was bored.
It felt like a long time since his
last adventure.

Suddenly, the Dragon Princess ran up to him.

"Yun, come with me! We must help my father, the Dragon King!"

Yun was scared but excited. Another dragon adventure!

The princess changed into a huge, white dragon. Yun climbed on her back and they flew over the lake.

"Where are we going?" asked Yun.

"To the Fire Demon's palace," said the princess. "He has stolen my father's magic pearl. Without the pearl, my father has no power. We must get it back!"

Chapter 2

Into the Volcano

They flew over the mountains to the top of an old volcano. In the middle of the volcano there was a blue lake.

"Down there!" said the princess.

Yun rubbed his dragon charm to use the power of breathing underwater. Then he and the princess dived down into the clear lake.

The water got warmer and warmer. After some time, they came to two passages. One of them led to the Fire Demon's palace. But which one?

One of the passages was glowing with red light. It looked dangerous.

"I think the Fire Demon lives down here," said Yun.

So Yun and the princess swam into the red passage. It got hotter and hotter. Then the passage twisted upwards, and the water got shallower and shallower.

At last there was no more water, and the passage led them to a large, dry cave. There, in the middle, was the Fire Demon's Ruby Palace.

Chapter 3
The Ruby Palace

Fierce fire spirits guarded the steps to the palace.

"Leave this to **me**!" roared the princess. Her roar was so fierce that it put the fire spirits out!

Yun and the princess flew up the steps and crept into the palace. After trying many doors, they found the Fire Demon's treasure room.

They could see him holding the Dragon
King's pearl. He was muttering, "With this
pearl I shall rule the Dragon King's kingdom."

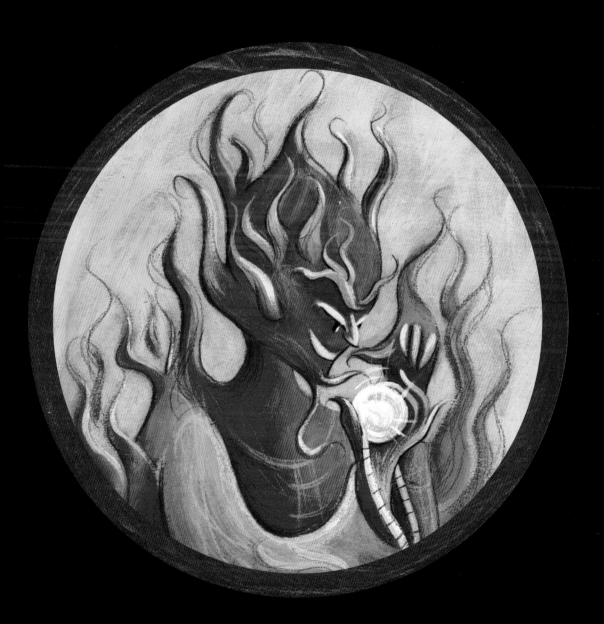

"No you won't," whispered Yun. He rushed into the room shouting, "Quick, run! The water is coming!" The Fire Demon jumped and the pearl slipped from his hand. Just in time, Yun leaped to catch the pearl.

The demon's eyes glowed red, and at once the fire spirit guards marched in. They came towards Yun and the princess, hissing, "You blew us out once. You will not do *that* again!"

"Just you wait and see!" laughed the princess. She let out a huge roar that sent a powerful jet of blue water over all of them.

Chapter 4

Escape!

Yun and the princess dashed out, leaving the dripping fire spirits and the Fire Demon behind. They flew towards the passage that led back to the lake. The fire spirits raced behind them. Yun and the princess dived into the passage just in time.

Yun and the princess rushed down the passage. They didn't look back. At last they swam up into the calm, blue waters of the lake.

The princess pulled Yun up through the water. He hung on tightly to the pearl. They burst up out of the lake and flew straight to the Dragon King's palace.

The Dragon King was pleased to see them – and his pearl. He blew on Yun's dragon charm.

"You have been brave, Yun," the Dragon King said. "So I have unlocked the next power – the power of flight. Use it well."